4-09

DATE DUE

BRODART

Cat. No. 23-221

THE ADVENTURES OF MARSHALL & ART

A Wheel Life Lesson

by Noel Gyro Potter
illustrated by Joseph Cannon

magic wagon

visit us at www.abdopublishing.com

*To Ryan, B & Harley. Throughout your lives, Dad & I are so proud
of you for always trying to help others. You are three decent,
caring young men and I love you endlessly.—NGP*

Published by Magic Wagon, a division of the ABDO Publishing Group, 8000 West 78th Street, Edina,
Minnesota 55439. Copyright © 2009 by Abdo Consulting Group, Inc. International copyrights reserved
in all countries.

Looking Glass Library™ is a trademark and logo of Magic Wagon.

Printed in the United States.

Written by Noel Gyro Potter
Illustrations by Joseph Cannon
Edited by Stephanie Hedlund and Rochelle Baltzer
Interior layout and design by Neil Klinepier
Cover design by Neil Klinepier

Library of Congress Cataloging-in-Publication Data

Potter, Noel Gyro.
  A wheel life lesson / written by Noel Gyro Potter ; illustrated by Joseph Cannon.
    p. cm. -- (The adventures of Marshall & Art)
  ISBN 978-1-60270-202-8
  I. Cannon, Joseph, 1958- ill. II. Title.
  PZ7.P8553Wh 2008
  [E]--dc22

                                                2008003630

It was a warm, breezy day, perfect for a picnic. And that was just what the James family was doing. Marshall and Art played a game of basketball. Their mom, dad, and little brother, Harley, sat in the shade with their dog, Rocket.

3

After a while, Marshall told Art, "I'm going to take a little break. I want to practice my karate kicks."

"Hurry up, okay? Corey and Brett just got here," Art said as he ran toward their friends.

Marshall began stretching. This would help make his kicks higher and stronger. Both Marshall and Art were talented, dedicated black belts. But, Marshall had a special dream—to someday be as good as his world champion dad, Johnny James!

Across the park, Marshall saw someone
watching him. It was a girl about his age
sitting in a wheelchair. Marshall thought he
had seen her before, but he couldn't quite
remember where or when.

"Hey, Marshall, are you done yet?" Art
hollered. "We're waiting for you."

"I'll be right there," Marshall answered.
He saw that the girl was still looking in his
direction, so he headed toward her.

As Marshall approached her, the girl quickly turned her wheelchair and started to move away.

"Wait a second!" Marshall called.

The girl stopped but didn't turn around. Marshall ran up to her.

"You go to Midland Park School, don't you?" he said. "I go there, too. My name is Marshall. Do you live near the park?"

"Why do you want to know? Are you a detective or something?" the girl snapped.

"No, I, uh, I just thought . . .," Marshall nervously stammered.

"Thought what? That I needed pity because I'm in a wheelchair? Or did you just want to tease me? How about 'Are you two-wheel or four-wheel drive?' or my favorite, 'Is it gas or electric?' I've heard them all and they're not funny," she said. She seemed angry and sad at the same time.

"I just thought that you might want some company," explained Marshall. "I guess some kids give you a hard time, huh? Maybe they don't realize how it feels to hear those things."

"Oh, I'm used to it by now," the girl answered. She looked shocked that Marshall wasn't going to tease her. "My name is Tate. I live just across the street from here."

When Tate relaxed, she was very pretty. But, Marshall still couldn't remember where he knew her from.

"My mom, dad, and little brothers, Art and Harley, are over there. Would you like to meet them?" Marshall offered.

"I know who your mom and dad are. I've been by your karate studio a thousand times watching the classes through the windows," Tate said.

"I knew I recognized you! How did you hurt yourself, I-I-I mean what happened to you?" asked Marshall, trying to hide how awkward he felt.

"What put me in this chair and why can't I use my legs anymore, you mean?" asked Tate.

"I guess, but you don't have to tell me if you don't want to. It's really none of my business. I probably shouldn't have even asked," Marshall said.

"When I was nine, my friends dared me to dive off of a dock. I didn't see the no diving sign, and I hit the bottom headfirst. My friends got a good laugh, but I got a wheelchair," said Tate sadly.

"Your parents must be so grateful that you survived! You could have died!" insisted Marshall. "Sometimes listening to our friends isn't such a great idea, is it?"

"Well, they said they were sorry. It was a dare that turned into a horrible accident. I know they didn't really mean to hurt me, and I knew better than to take a dare," admitted Tate.

Marshall wanted to cheer Tate up, so he said, "How about it, Tate? Do you want to meet my family?"

"I guess I could. It's not like I'm going to be late for a track meet or dance class," joked Tate.

Marshall saw a hint of a smile on Tate's face. He was relieved that she wasn't as angry as she'd seemed.

"Hey, Art! I want you to meet someone!" Marshall called. Art, Corey, and Brett ran toward Marshall and Tate.

"This is Tate. Tate, this is my brother, Art, and our friends, Corey and Brett," Marshall said.

Art was the first to speak up. "Hi, Tate. Are you ready to play ball now, Marshall?"

"How about a game of five-way ringtoss instead?" Marshall said as he winked at Art. Art quickly understood.

"Good idea. Are you guys up for it?" Art asked.

In no time, all five kids were playing, talking, and laughing. Marshall was glad Tate was having fun instead of sitting alone.

When it was time for a break, Marshall offered to push Tate up the small hill where his parents sat.

"Mom, Dad, this is my friend, Tate," Marshall said proudly.

"I've seen you at our karate studio many times, young lady. I wish some of our students watched as closely as you do!" Johnny said. "We're very happy to finally meet you!"

"I wish I could do karate! I've always dreamed of becoming a black belt just like you, Mrs. James. Now I can't," Tate said.

"Of course you can! You can learn to use ancient weapons and many self-defense moves right from your wheelchair. There's a lot you can do! But first you have to stop saying 'can't,' okay?" encouraged Marti.

"But, what if the kids make fun of me because I'm at a karate studio in a wheelchair? That seems kind of odd, doesn't it?" Tate asked.

"The kids in our studio are taught respect for situations just like yours," Johnny said. "There are lots of kids with special needs there and we all work together."

"You'll be fine! You can trust us, Tate!" urged Marshall.

"This is great! I'm going to go home right now and tell my parents! Thank you for everything! Marshall, I'll see you at school tomorrow," Tate said.

"Okay! I'm really glad we finally met, Tate. See you later," said Marshall.

"Marshall, we're proud of you for introducing yourself to Tate. Today could have been another day she spent sitting all alone. Instead, you made a new friend," said Marti.

"You're right, Mom. And Tate made a lot more friends, too!" Marshall said as the James family headed home.

"Dare" to Be Different

Sometimes it is fun to dare your friends or accept a dare to do dangerous or silly things. But those dares can lead to severe consequences, such as injuries or trouble with the law. Daring someone doesn't prove anything. Use your courage to say no to a challenge to do something you know you shouldn't do. Dare yourself to be brave by doing the right thing and say no to dares!

Children:
- Don't let your friends talk you into doing things you know you shouldn't do!
- Be strong. Always remember it is okay to say no to your friends when you're tempted to do something that doesn't feel right, may be dangerous, or is wrong.
- Share your feelings and temptations with an adult. Adults understand giving and taking dares—they were a kid once, too!

Adults:
- Surprisingly, children are often bullied by friends that they know and trust. Remind children not to let their friends encourage them to do things they shouldn't do, especially while feeling pressured on a dare.
- Have regular conversations with a child about the pleasant and unpleasant events of their day. Your genuine interest will welcome him or her to communicate with you so you can recognize a problem before it's too late.
- Share similar childhood experiences. Children feel great relief and enjoy learning that adults have gone through the very same rites of passage that they are experiencing!